WEE RHYMES

WEE RHYMES

Baby's First Poetry Book

Jane Yolen

· ILLUSTRATED BY ·

Jane Dyer

A Paula Wiseman Book

SIMON & SCHUSTER BOOKS FOR YOUNG READERS

NEW YORK   LONDON   TORONTO   SYDNEY   NEW DELHI

SIMON & SCHUSTER BOOKS FOR YOUNG READERS
An imprint of Simon & Schuster Children's Publishing Division
1230 Avenue of the Americas, New York, New York 10020
SIMON & SCHUSTER BOOKS FOR YOUNG READERS is a trademark of Simon & Schuster, Inc.
For information about special discounts for bulk purchases,
please contact Simon & Schuster Special Sales at 1-866-506-1949 or business@simonandschuster.com.
The Simon & Schuster Speakers Bureau can bring authors to your live event. For more information or to book an event,
contact the Simon & Schuster Speakers Bureau at 1-866-248-3049 or visit our website at www.simonspeakers.com.
Book design by Laurent Linn
The text for this book is set in Brinar Pro.
The illustrations for this book are drawn in pencil and painted in watercolors.
Manufactured in China • 1212 SCP
2 4 6 8 10 9 7 5 3 1
Library of Congress Cataloging-in-Publication Data
Yolen, Jane.
Wee rhymes : baby's first poetry book / Jane Yolen ; illustrated by Jane
Dyer.—1st ed.
p. cm.
"A Paula Wiseman Book."
Summary: A collection of nursery rhymes, most original but some from
Mother Goose, divided into sections celebrating all of the special moments
in a baby's day, from wake-up time to bedtime.
ISBN 978-1-4169-4898-8 (hardcover)
1. Nursery rhymes. 2. Children's poetry. [1. Nursery rhymes.] I. Dyer,
Jane, ill. II. Title.
PZ8.3.Y76Wee 2013
[398.8]—dc23
2012015136

Editor's Note: All poems are created by Jane Yolen except when noted as traditional Mother Goose rhymes.

To my six grandchildren: Glendon, Maddison,
Alison, David, Caroline, and Amelia—

—J. Y.

For Clementine, Blue, and Violet—with love from Grandma Jane

—J. D.

CONTENTS

A Note from Two Grandmothers

If you add our grandchildren together, we have nine. Jane Y (Nana) has six: five girls and a boy. Jane D (Grandma) has three: two girls and a boy. We sing to them, read to them, make up stories and poems with them, do art projects, bake and dance and cuddle, and when they were tiny, we watched them breathe as they slept.

We both believe that literature begins in the cradle. Rhymes are our earliest cultural artifacts. Children who are given poetry early will have a fullness inside. Mother Goose rhymes, baby verse—that kind of singsong, sing-along rhythm—is as important as a heartbeat. Add pictures to them, and you have the whole early childhood package. Just add the love.

That is why we have made this book for all you parents, grandparents, godparents, aunts, uncles—the grown-ups—to use with your wee ones, in case any of you are shy about making or finding rhymes to recite. So put a child on your lap or snuggle close, and make that cozy time, that cooing time, a rhyme-and-picture time as well.

—Jane Yolen and Jane Dyer

THE ROSE IS RED

The rose is red,

The violet's blue,

Pinks are sweet,

And so are you!

—MOTHER GOOSE

SO SWEET, SO NEAT

So sweet, so neat,
So daffodil and daisy.
Lying cozy in your crib
And acting very lazy.

So sweet, so neat,
So lavender and lily.
Hair like the softest silk,
And a smile so silly.

COOZIES, COZIES

Coozies, cozies,

Feet and toesies.

Giggle, wiggle,

Up you go!

FIVE LITTLE FINGERS

Five little fingers

On each hand.

Here's a kiss.

There's a miss.

Isn't baby grand.

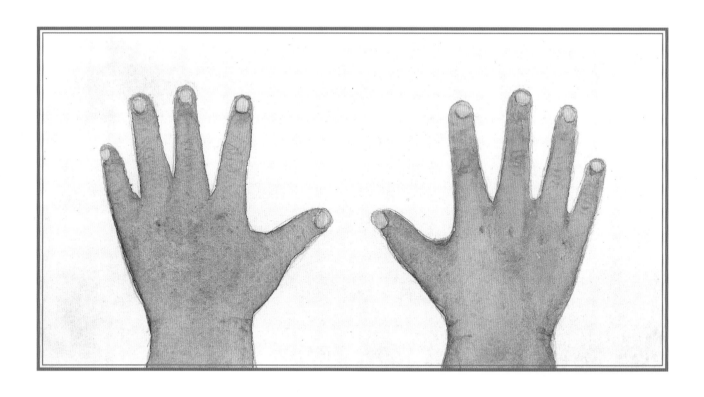

KISSES

Kiss the toes,

Kiss the nose,

Kiss the lips and hair.

Now we're giving baby kisses

Every, *every*where!

HUGS

Mama's hug is gentle,

Daddy's hug is long,

Granddad's hug

Is warm as a rug,

And Grandma's comes with a song.

TICKLE SONG

Tickles are butterfly wings.

They flutter and butter your skin.

They flit all about,

Make giggles come out,

Then let all the loving come in.

BELLY BUTTON MUSIC

Lips to belly button,

Blow, blow, blow.

Can you hear that belly button go?

Brrr-rup, brrr-rup.

Such a silly song.

Let's play the belly button

All . . . *brrr-rup* . . . day . . . *brrr-rup* . . . long.

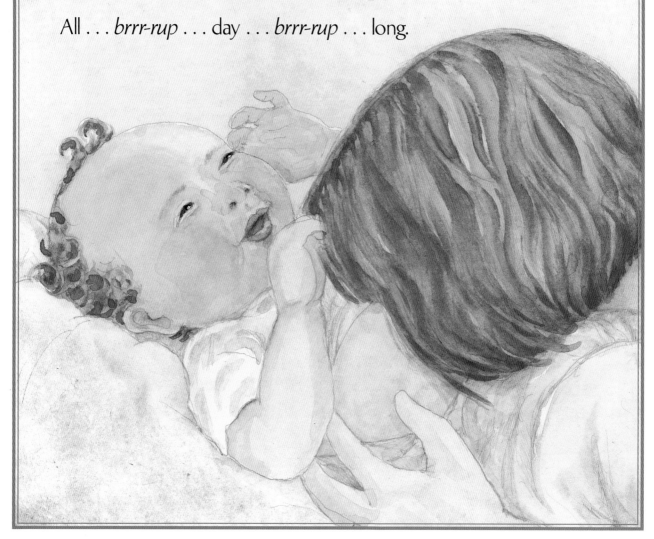

UP, UP, UP

Pat your hands, make them clap,

Sitting cozy in my lap.

Be my bottle, be my cup,

I'm going to eat you up, up, up!

UP, LITTLE BABY

Up, little baby, stand up clear;

Mother will hold you, do not fear;

Dimple and smile, and chuckle and crow!

There, little baby, now you know!

—MOTHER GOOSE

BABY HAS THE WIGGLES

Baby has the wiggles.

Baby can't sit still.

Baby has the giggles.

Baby has a will.

BOUNCING ON MY KNEE

Here we come from Dreamland,

There we go to town.

Baby riding on my knee,

Up, up, up—and down.

ALL FALL DOWN

Upsie, daisy,

Oh so crazy.

Look out—all fall down.

Pick you up

And dust you off,

And kiss away that frown.

WALKING

One step, then another,

Toe and heel go we,

Round about the bedroom,

Soon you'll walk with me.

One step, then another,

Toe and heel we go,

Round about the bedroom,

Fast, fast, fast—and slow.

ALL BY YOURSELF

You can put your shoes on,
Shoes on, shoes on,
You can put your shoes on,
Soon you will be dressed.

Shirt and pants and shoes on.
Can you do the rest?

SPECIAL BLANKIE

Raggedy,

Saggedy,

Baggedy,

Worn.

You got it

The afternoon

That you

Were born.

It was silky

And shiny.

So soft

And not torn.

You carry it

With you

From bedtime

Till morn.

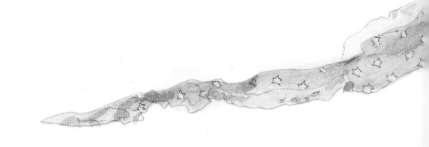

PAT-A-CAKE

Pat-a-cake, pat-a-cake,

Baker's man,

Bake me a cake

As fast as you can;

Prick it and pat it,

And mark it with *B*,

And put it in the oven

For Baby and me.

—MOTHER GOOSE

BABY'S BIB

Baby's in the cradle,

Baby's in the crib,

Baby's in the high chair

Wearing Baby's bib.

BREAKFAST TIME

Here's a little cup.

Here's a little spoon.

Eat up all the food;

You will be full soon.

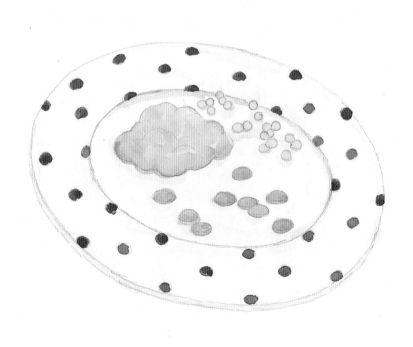

MAMA PICK UP

Baby threw his spoon down.

Mama picked it up.

Next he threw his plate down

And his plastic cup.

Baby clapped his hands,

And waited for some more.

"No," said Mama,

And left them on the floor.

YUM-YUMS

Yum, yum for the tum.

Big smiles from little groans.

A spoon of peach, a spoon of pear,

And milk makes mighty bones.

SWEET

Sugar is sweet but you are sweeter.

Sprinkle you in my tea.

One kiss here and one kiss there,

No one is dearer to me.

Honey is sweet but you are sweeter.

Spread you all over my toast.

One kiss here and one kiss there,

And I love you the most.

MILK

Glorious milk, so clean and white.

I wish I could, I wish I might

Take a picture and laugh, laugh, laugh

When baby has a milk mustache.

MUNCH, MUNCH

Munch, munch,

Crisp, crunch,

Which do you like better—

Breakfast or lunch?

OOPS, WHOOPS

Oops, whoops,
Down the cup goes.
Now you have milk
All over your toes.

Now, little sweetling,
Don't you yowl.
Here comes Daddy
With a great big towel.

GIRLS AND BOYS, COME OUT TO PLAY

Girls and boys, come out to play.

The moon is shining as bright as day.

Come with a whoop, come with a call,

Come with a good will or not at all.

—MOTHER GOOSE

BUILDING BLOCKS

Make a tower,

High, high, high,

Till its top

Can touch the sky.

Twice as fast

As it arose,

SMASH, *CRASH*,

Down it goes!

BABY'S BIG TRUCK

Your truck is big.

Your truck is red.

You keep it in

A little shed.

It has a bell,

A siren, too.

Let's hear it go,

Whoooooo, whooooo!

TEDDY

Big brown ears.

Big brown nose.

Big brown everywhere,

I suppose.

Love him up.

Love him down.

Love him everywhere,

Brown, brown, brown.

YOUR LITTLE DOLLY

Your little dolly
Has big blue eyes.
She closes them
And then she cries.

She opens them
And calls your name
Whenever you play
The Mama game.

RATTLES, DRUMS, AND BELLS

Play with the rattle.

SHAKE! SHAKE! SHAKE!

Not so hard

That it could break.

Beat on the drum.

BOOM! BOOM! BOOM!

A sound that fills

The living room.

Clang the bells.

DING! DANG! DONG!

Now we're playing

A happy song.

SITTING IN THE QUIET CHAIR

When you're bad
And make a riot,
You must go
And be real quiet.

There's a place,
And there's a chair.
And when you're bad,
You must sit there.

SOMETIMES MOMMY, SOMETIMES DADDY

When you fall,

When you cry,

Sometimes Mommy

Lifts you high.

When you yell

Or drop your cup,

Sometimes Daddy

Picks you up.

When you're good,

I know it's true,

Sometimes the only one

who knows—

Is you.

THIS LITTLE PIG

This little pig went to market.

This little pig stayed home.

This little pig had roast beef.

And this little pig had none.

And this little pig said,

"Wee, wee, wee!" all the way home.

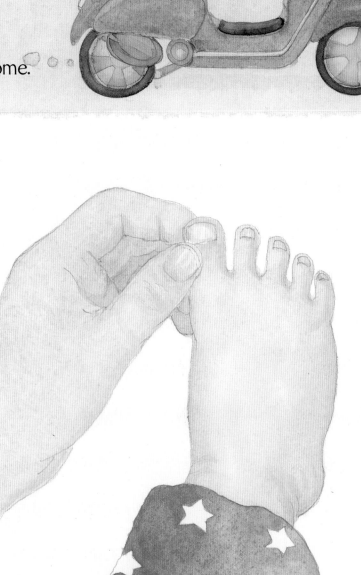

—MOTHER GOOSE

HOLDING ON

Daddy holds your hand real tight,

One step, two skips, a slide.

Daddy and you on the zebra line

Safe to the other side.

PIGGYBACK

Piggyback ride, piggyback ride,

We'll carry you over to that other side.

Daddy can do it, and Mommy can too.

Giddyup, baby, we'll piggyback you.

STROLLER ROLLER

Your stroller rolls along-long-long,

And as it rolls, you sing this song:

The cars go *beep*!

The trucks go *zoom*!

The people *shout*!

The buses *boom*!

And we go *whee-whee-whee-whee-whee*,

All the way home.

STREET RULES

Go is when the light turns green,
But stop is when it's red.
You must look from side to side
Before you go ahead.

You mustn't run, but mustn't linger;
Skipping is for fools.
When you go across the street,
You have to know the rules.

LET'S GO

Let's go to the supermarket,

Ride down every aisle,

Wave at all the shoppers,

Make everybody smile.

Let's pay them at the counter.

I'll help you count to ten.

Let's take our packages all home,

Then let's go back again!

Again!

WHEELS

How many wheels

Go round and round?

Some make noise,

Some make no sound.

Some are fast

And some are slow.

Can you count them

As they go?

MULBERRY BUSH

Here we go round

The mulberry bush,

The mulberry bush,

The mulberry bush.

Here we go round the mulberry bush,

So early in the morning.

—MOTHER GOOSE

BABY IN THE GRASS

Barefoot—grass between the toes.

Belly down—grass up the nose.

LYING IN THE GRASS

Let's lie on our backs
And look at the sky,
Counting the birds
As they all fly by.

Little birds, big birds,
Red, blue, and black.
Let's hope that some of them
Fly right back.

TURN AROUND

Turn around, turn around,

Make the ground spin.

The one who goes fastest is

The one who will win.

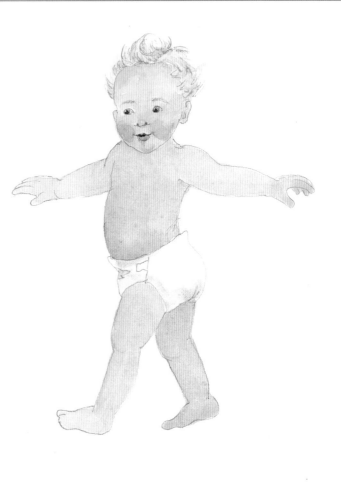

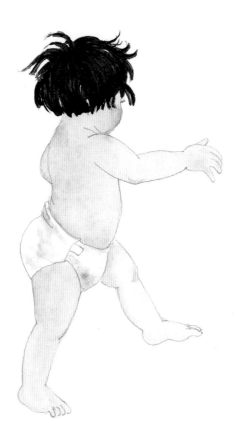

YOU HAVE A SWING

You have a swing
And you can fly,
Both feet forward
To the sky.

When the swing
Begins to slow,
The ground sneaks up
From down below.

MY SLIDE

You have a slide
Where you go fast,
Both feet forward
Into the grass.

SANDBOX

So many grains of sand.

So few ticks of time.

Shovel them here, pat them there.

Some are yours, some mine.

So many grains of sand.

The ticks of time are gone.

And half your grains of sand

Are now on Daddy's lawn.

GO TO BED, TOM

Go to bed, Tom.

Go to bed, Tom!

Tired or not, Tom,

Go to bed, Tom.

—MOTHER GOOSE

NAP TIME

You say you're not sleepy.

You say it's not dark.

You say that you want to

Go walk in the park.

You say you're not tired.

You say it's too soon.

You say that you only sleep

When there's a moon.

You say you want water.

You cry, "Where's my blankie?"

You snuffle and whuffle

And ask for a hankie.

You say, "Want a story."

You beg, "Stay with me."

And just when I'm ready to give in . . .

   Zzzzzzzzzzzz.

LITTLE ZZZZS, BIG ZZZZS

Little zzzzs, big zzzzs,

Hiccups, sigh.

Bad dreams, wild screams,

You start to cry.

Little zzzzs, big zzzzs,

In a while,

Dreams are happy ones.

Then you smile.

WHO IS SLEEPING?

Dolly is, eyes open wide.

Teddy is, upon his side.

I am snoozing, book on lap.

But Baby doesn't want to nap.

BABY SNORES

Listen to the baby's snore,

ZZZZZZZZZZZZZZZZZZ.

Singing through the open door,

ZZZZZZZZZZZZZZZZZZ.

Like a little buzzing fly,

ZZZZZZZZZZZZZZZZZZZ.

Will you wake him?

No, not I.

ZZZZZZZZZZZZZZZZZZZ.

EVERYBODY NEEDS A TEDDY SOMETIMES

Everybody needs a teddy sometimes.

Everybody needs a hug or two.

Everybody needs a teddy one time,

To hug and snuggle up right next to you.

Here's a binkie; that'll stop your crying.

Here's a tissue; wipe away those tears.

Here's a teddy ready to be trying

To ease your troubles and to calm your fears.

'Cause everybody needs a teddy sometimes,

Everybody needs a hug or two.

Everybody needs a teddy one time,

To hug and snuggle up right next to you.

SIPPITY SUP

Sippity sup, sippity sup.

Bread and milk from a china cup.

Bread and milk from a bright silver spoon

Made of a piece of the bright silver moon.

Sippity sup, sippity sup,

Sippity, sippity sup.

—MOTHER GOOSE

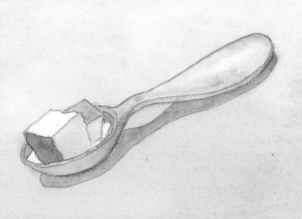

DINNERTIME

Who's not hungry,
Not a bit?
Who wants to run,
Not table-sit?

Who says that he
Has just got up,
Then happily drinks milk
From his sippy cup?

One for Baby.
Two for me.
We only eat
When we're hung-*a*-ry!

SPOON

Man in the moon,

He has a spoon.

He snacks upon the stars.

He crunches them

And munches them

And keeps the rest in jars.

GREENS

Peas are greens,

Cucumbers, too.

Lettuce, beans—

But you like blue.

SAYING BANANAS

Do you love bananananas whole?

Do you love bananananas chopped?

Cause when you try to say,

"Bananananas,"

You really don't know when you're s'posed to stop.

THE FOOD TRAIN

Here comes the engine.

Open wide.

The train choo-chews

The food inside.

And last of all,

A drink of juice

Delivered by

The food caboose.

RUB-A-DUB-DUB

Rub-a-dub-dub,

Three men in a tub,

And who do you think they be?

The butcher, the baker,

The candlestick maker,

Who all set out to sea.

—MOTHER GOOSE

TIME FOR A BATH

Dirt in your fingernails,

Dirt in your hair.

You've got grass stains

Everywhere.

Time for a bath.

In you go.

Splish and splash.

Now, don't be slow.

SCRUB-A-DUB

Scrub-a-dub

In the tub.

Clean up

And then,

Tomorrow

You can get

All dirty

Again.

IN THE TUB

You get in the water,

Pretend you can float,

Along with three duckies,

A turtle, a boat.

Quack say the duckies.

The boat goes *whooo-whooo*.

The turtle just sinks

With a bubble or two.

SOAP DRAGONS

You are a soapy superman
And when you're in the tub,
You like to do much more than bathe
And give yourself a scrub.

You like to fight soap dragons.
You like to watch them *pop!*
Then soapy feathers float around
Into the bathtub slop.

And when you get out on the mat
I have to hose you there.
Because there's still a lot of dragon
Stuck up in your hair.

HOLE IN THE BATHTUB

I wash the dirt off from your face,

Your hands, your feet, your hair.

And when you get out of the tub,

You leave the dirt right there.

But later on, when you're in bed,

I bet that you suppose

That down the hole that's in the tub

Is where the dirt all goes.

You think it flows outside where we

Are going the next day.

That's where you'll get all dirty—

So muddy, gross, and dirty—

And then you'll bring the dirt back home

And wash it all away.

TOWEL

You're wrapped in a towel,
And now that you're dry,
Speak up loud and clear:
"What a clean child am I."

BRUSHING TEETH

Baby doesn't have a lot—

A few below, a few on top.

But brushing them will keep them strong

Until the rest all come along.

PAJAMAS

Your pajamas are covered with horses.

Your pajamas are colored bright red.

Your pajamas have feet that keep you real warm

Whenever they stick out of bed.

ROCK-A-BYE, BABY

Rock-a-bye, baby,

in the treetop.

When the wind blows,

the cradle will rock.

When the bough breaks,

the cradle will fall,

And down will come baby,

cradle and all.

—Mother Goose

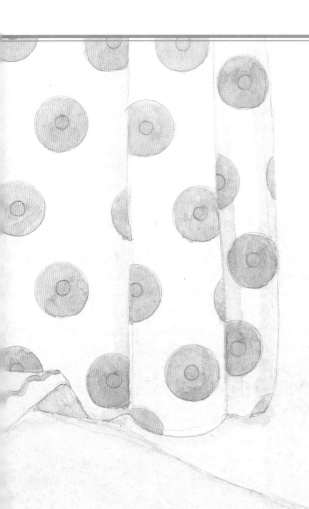

TIME FOR BED

It's time to go to bed.
The stars are winking on,
Like little sparkling fireflies,
And soon day will be gone.

Now, when your room is dark,
You'll look out at the sight,
Happy that you have the stars
To be your own night-light.

READ TO ME: A CHILD TO MOMMY

"Read to me riddles and read to me rhymes,

Read to me stories of magical times.

Read to me tales about castles and kings.

Read to me stories of fabulous things.

Read to me pirates and read to me knights.

Read to me dragons and dragonback fights.

Read to me spaceships and cowboys and then

When you are finished—please read them again."

READING TO BEAR

Your teddy bear,
With one chewed ear,
Loves to sit beside you
Here.

He likes that you
Read him a book.
He sits quite still,
And has a look.

Your teddy bear,
With blinkless eye,
Thinks you can read.
I wonder why.

That's because
When you're in bed,
You read him *pictures* there
Instead.

NIGHT WORRIES

Bear in the closet,

Don't growl.

Wolves under the bed,

Don't howl.

Troll behind the door,

Don't roar.

At least not before

Baby is asleep.

SWEET DREAMS

If dreams were cotton candy,

If dreams were sugar fluff,

We'd spend our nights in dreaming

And never get enough.

GOOD NIGHT

Good night, sleep tight,

Happy dreams

Till morning light.

Then . . .

Coozies, cozies,

Feet and toesies.

Giggle, wiggle,

Up you go

Again!